The Brave Baby

Written by Malachy Doyle
Illustrated by Richard Johnson

The Indian chief was brave and fierce,
so many people were afraid of him.

But a wise old woman said,
"I know someone who is not afraid of you."

The Indian chief was surprised.

"Who is this man?" he cried. "Show him to me!"

4

The old woman took him to her tent.

"Where is this man?" said the chief.
"I cannot see him."

"It is not a man," said the old woman.
"It is Wasso, the baby girl."
Wasso sat on a blanket, playing with a stick.

"Why is this baby not afraid of me?"
said the chief.
"Everyone is afraid of me!"

"Come here, child!" he cried.
But Wasso only smiled at him.

"Come here, I said!"
The chief was cross with the little girl.

Wasso stopped smiling and
looked up at the chief.

"You must do as I say, child!" cried the chief. Wasso looked at the man who was shouting at her, and she began to cry.

Wasso cried and she cried, but
she still would not go to the chief.

So the chief began to dance.
It was a special dance –
a dance to make people do as he said.

Wasso stopped crying.
She liked the dance.
She looked up at the chief and she smiled.

The chief did another dance,
to make her come to him.
But Wasso only laughed.

The chief danced some more, but still
the baby would not do as he said.
Still she would not go to him.

The chief danced and danced.
Wasso smiled and laughed ...

... and then she fell asleep.

18

"You see," said the old woman to the chief.
"Here is someone who is not afraid of you."

"You are right," said the chief.
"Wasso is braver than me.
She is a very brave baby."
20

The chief was too tired to be angry any more.
He liked the brave baby.
He lay down in the tent
and fell fast asleep.

The Brave Baby Storyboard

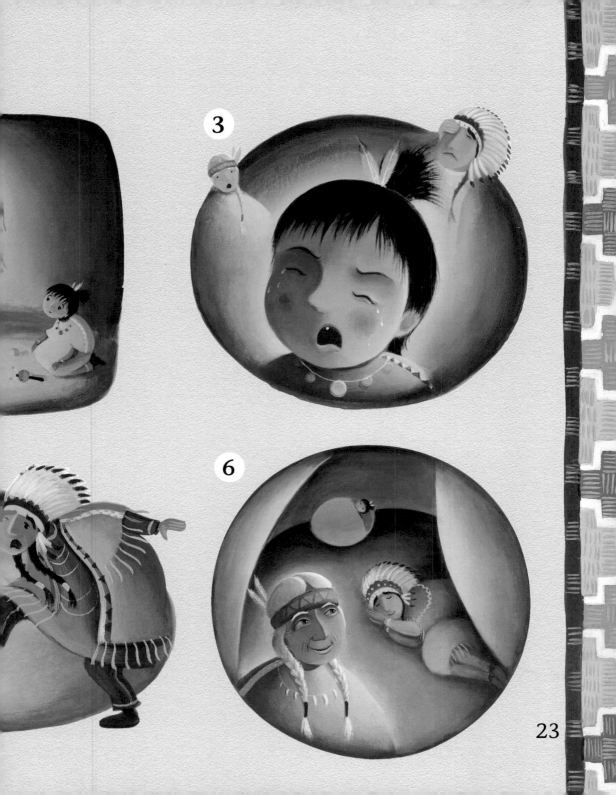

3

6

23

✿: Ideas for guided reading ✿:

Learning objectives: Discussing how characters are described; making predictions based on an understanding of character; reading words with initial consonant clusters; acting out stories using different voices for characters

Curriculum links: Geography: Where in the world is Barnaby Bear?

Interest words: fierce, afraid, surprised

Word count: 321

Getting started

- Ask the children to look at the front cover and discuss what kind of story this is. Introduce the main characters and setting and read the title.

- Look through the book at the pictures and words up to p12. Tell the children that you won't go to the end of the story yet so they can predict what will happen.

- Ask the children about the setting and draw on any knowledge of Native American culture.

- Find examples of words with initial consonant clusters, e.g. *playing*, *blanket*, *smiled*. Ask the children to point to and read the initial consonants then read the whole word.

- Read p2. What words are used to describe the chief?

Reading and responding

- Ask the children to read independently until p12 and then tell a partner what they think will happen next. Ask the children to think about what kind of person the chief is.

- Look out for fluent and well-phrased reading using grammar and punctuation and following print with eyes rather than finger pointing.

- Some prompts for challenging vocabulary could include: *Can you see that word again (for a repeated word); Look at the beginning/end of the word and see if you can work it out.*